First published 2011 by Nosy Crow Ltd
The Crow's Nest, 11 The Chandlery
50 Westminster Bridge Road
London SE1 7QY
www.nosycrow.com

ISBN 978 0 85763 005 6 (HB)

A CIP catalogue record for this book is available from the British Library.

Printed in China

1 3 5 7 9 8 6 4 2

Pip and Posy

The Super Scooter

Axel Scheffler

nosy crow

Pip was riding on
his scooter.

He went **up** . . .   he went **down** . . .

he **even** did tricks on it.

Just then, Posy appeared.

Posy really liked Pip's scooter.

She wanted to ride on it a lot.

So Posy snatched the scooter and scooted away as fast as she could!

Pip felt **very** cross.

Posy had never been on a scooter before,
but she thought it looked quite easy.

She went up . . .

she went down . . .

. . . she even **tried** to do a trick on it.

Careful, Posy!

Then Posy fell off the scooter.

Oh dear!

Poor Posy!

She hurt her knee and was very sad.

So Pip looked after Posy and her sore leg.

"I'm sorry for taking your scooter, Pip," said Posy.

"Thank you for looking after me."

Pip and Posy had a big hug.

They went to play in the sand

where it was nice and soft.

And then they went
home for tea.

Hooray!